HORRiD HENRY
Ghosts and Ghouls

Francesca Simon spent her childhood on the beach
in California, and then went to Yale and Oxford
Universities to study medieval history and literature.
She now lives in London with her family. She has written
over 50 books and won the Children's Book of the Year
at the Galaxy British Book Awards for *Horrid Henry
and the Abominable Snowman*.

Tony Ross is one of the most popular and successful
of all children's illustrators, with almost 50 picture books
to his name. He has also produced line drawings for
many fiction titles, for authors such as David Walliams,
Enid Blyton, Astrid Lindgren and many more.

For a complete list of **Horrid Henry** titles
see the end of the book, or visit
www.horridhenry.co.uk
or
www.hachettechildrens.co.uk

HORRID HENRY
Ghosts and Ghouls

Francesca Simon
Illustrated by Tony Ross

Orion
Children's Books

ORION CHILDREN'S BOOKS
This collection first published in Great Britain in 2018
by Hodder and Stoughton
1 3 5 7 9 10 8 6 4 2

A CIP catalogue record for this book
is available from the British Library.

ISBN 978 1 5101 0518 8

Printed and bound in Great Britain by Clays Ltd, Elcograf S.p.A.

The paper and board used in this book are from
well-managed forests and other responsible sources.

Orion Children's Books
An imprint of
Hachette Children's Books
Part of Hodder and Stoughton
Carmelite House
50 Victoria Embankment
London EC4Y 0DZ

An Hachette UK Company
www.hachette.co.uk
www.hachettechildrens.co.uk
www.horridhenry.co.uk

CONTENTS

HORRID HENRY
AND THE
MUMMY'S CURSE

Tiptoe. Tiptoe. Tiptoe.

Horrid Henry crept down the hall. The coast was clear. Mum and Dad were in the garden, and Peter was playing at Tidy Ted's.

Tee hee, thought Henry, then darted into Perfect Peter's room and shut the door.

There it was. Sitting unopened on Peter's shelf. The grossest, yuckiest, most stomach-curdling kit Henry had ever seen. A brand-new, deluxe 'Curse of the Mummy' kit, complete with a plastic body to mummify, mummy-wrapping

1

gauze, curse book, amulets and, best of all, removable mummy organs to put in a canopic jar. Peter had won it at the 'Meet a Real Mummy' exhibition at the museum, but he'd never even played with it once.

Of course, Henry wasn't allowed into Peter's bedroom without permission. He was also not allowed to play with Peter's toys. This was so unfair, Henry could hardly believe it. True, he wouldn't let Peter touch his Boom-Boom Basher, his Goo-Shooter, or his Dungeon Drink kit. In fact, since Henry refused

2

to share *any* of his toys with Peter, Mum
had forbidden Henry to play with any of
Peter's toys – or else.

Henry didn't care – Perfect Peter
had boring baby toys – until, that is, he
brought home the mummy kit. Henry
had ached to play with it. And now was
his chance.

Horrid Henry tore off the wrapping,
and opened the box.

WOW! So gross! Henry felt a delicious
shiver. He loved mummies. What could
be more thrilling than looking at an
ancient, wrapped-up DEAD body? Even
a pretend one was wonderful. And now
he had hours of fun ahead of him.

Pitter-patter! Pitter-patter! Pitter-patter!

Oh help, someone was coming up the
stairs! Horrid Henry shoved the mummy
kit behind him as Peter's bedroom door
swung open and Perfect Peter strolled in.

'Out of my way, worm!' shouted Henry.

Perfect Peter slunk off. Then he stopped.

'Wait a minute,' he said. 'You're in *my* room! You can't order me out of my own room!'

'Oh yeah?' blustered Henry.

'Yeah!' said Peter.

'You're supposed to be at Ted's,' said Henry, trying to distract him.

'He got sick,' said Peter. He stepped closer. 'And you're playing with my kit! You're not allowed to play with any of my things! Mum said so! I'm going to tell her right now!'

Uh oh. If Peter told on him Henry would be in big trouble. Very big trouble. Henry had to save himself, fast. He had two choices. He could leap on Peter and throttle him. Or he could use weasel words.

'I wasn't playing with it,' said Henry smoothly. 'I was trying to protect you.'

'No you weren't,' said Peter. 'I'm telling.'

'I was, too,' said Henry. 'I was trying to protect you from the Mummy's Curse.'

Perfect Peter headed for the door. Then he stopped.

'What curse?' said Peter.

'The curse which turns people into mummies!' said Henry desperately.

'There's no such thing,' said Peter.

'Wanna bet?' said Henry. 'Everyone knows about the mummy's curse! They take on the shape of someone familiar but really, they're mummies! They could be your cat—'

'Fluffy?' said Peter. 'Fluffy, a mummy?'

Henry looked at fat Fluffy snoring peacefully on a cushion.

'Even Fluffy,' said Henry. 'Or Dad. Or Me. Or you.'

'I'm not a mummy,' said Peter.

'Or even—' Henry paused melo-dramatically and then whispered, 'Mum.'

'Mum, a mummy?' gasped Peter.

'Yup,' said Henry. 'But don't worry.
You help me draw some Eyes of Horus.
They'll protect us against . . . her.'

'She's not a mummy,' said Peter.

'That's what she wants us to think,'
whispered Henry. 'It's all here in the
Mummy curse book.' He waved the
book in front of Peter. 'Don't you think
the mummy on the cover resembles
you-know-who?'

'No,' said Peter.

'Watch,' said Horrid Henry. He
grabbed a pencil.

'Don't draw on a book!' squeaked
Peter.

Henry ignored him and drew glasses
on the mummy.

'How about now?' he asked.

Peter stared. Was it his imagination or
did the mummy look a little familiar?

'I don't believe you,' said Peter. 'I'm
going straight down to ask Mum.'

'But that's the worst thing you could
do!' shouted Henry.

'I don't care,' said Peter. Down he went.

Henry was sunk. Mum would probably cancel his birthday party when Peter blabbed. And he'd never even had a chance to play with the mummy kit! It was so unfair.

Mum was reading on the sofa.

'Mum,' said Peter, 'Henry says you're a mummy.'

Mum looked puzzled.

'Of course I'm a mummy,' she said.

'What?' said Peter.

'I'm your mummy,' said Mum, with a smile.

Peter took a step back.

'I don't want you to be a mummy,' said Peter.

'But I am one,' said Mum. 'Now come and give me a hug.'

'No!' said Peter.

'Let me wrap my arms around you,' said Mum.

'NO WRAPPING!' squealed Peter. 'I want my mummy!'

'But I'm your mummy,' said Mum.

'I know!' squeaked Peter. 'Keep away, you . . . Mummy!'

Perfect Peter staggered up the stairs
to Henry.

'It's true,' he gasped. 'She said she
was a mummy.'

'She did?' said Henry.

'Yes,' said Peter. 'What are we going
to do?'

'Don't worry, Peter,' said Henry.
'We can free her from the curse.'

'How?' breathed Peter.

Horrid Henry pretended to consult
the curse book.

'First we must sacrifice to the
Egyptian gods Osiris and Hroth,' said
Henry.

'Sacrifice?' said Peter.

'They like cat guts, and stuff like that,'
said Henry.

'No!' squealed Peter. 'Not . . . Fluffy!'

'However,' said Henry, leafing through
the curse book, 'marbles are also acceptable

as an offering.'

Perfect Peter ran to his toybox and scooped up a handful of marbles.

'Now fetch me some loo roll,' added Henry.

'Loo roll?' said Peter.

'Do not question the priest of Anubis!' shrieked Henry.

Perfect Peter fetched the loo roll.

'We must wrap Fluffy in the sacred bandages,' said Henry. 'He will be our messenger between this world and the next.'

'Meoww,' said Fluffy, as he was wrapped from head to tail in loo paper.

'Now you,' said Henry.

12

'Me?' squeaked Peter.

'Yes,' said Henry. 'Do you want to free Mum from the mummy's curse?'

Peter nodded.

'Then you must stand still and be quiet for thirty minutes,' said Henry. That should give him plenty of time to have a go with the mummy kit.

He started wrapping Peter. Round and round and round and round went the loo roll until Peter was tightly trussed from head to toe.

Henry stepped back to admire his work. Goodness, he was a brilliant mummy-maker! Maybe that's what he should be when he grew up. Henry, the Mummy-Maker. Henry, World's Finest Mummy-Maker. Henry, Mummy-Maker to the Stars. Yes, it certainly had a ring to it.

'You're a fine-looking mummy, Peter,' said Henry. 'I'm sure you'll be made very welcome in the next world.'

'Huuunh?' said Peter.

'Silence!'ordered Henry. 'Don't move. Now I must utter the sacred spell. By the powers of Horus, Morus, Borus and Stegosaurus,' intoned Henry, making up all the Egyptian sounding names he could.

'Stegosaurus?' mumbled Peter.

'Whatever!' snapped Henry. 'I call on the scarab! I call on Isis! Free Fluffy from the mummy's curse. Free Peter from the mummy's curse. Free Mum from the mummy's curse. Free— '

'What on earth is going on in here?' shrieked Mum, bursting through the door. 'You horrid boy! What have you done to Peter? And what have you done to poor Fluffy?'

15

'Meoww,' yowled Fluffy.

'Mummy!' squealed Perfect Peter.

Eowww, gross! thought Horrid Henry, opening up the plastic mummy body and placing the organs in the canopic jar.

The bad news was that Henry had been banned from watching TV for a week. The good news was that Perfect Peter had said he never wanted to see that horrible mummy kit again.

Henry's Halloween Howlers

What do witches
use in the summer?
Suntan potion.

What do you call an alien
with three eyes?
Aliiien.

What happens when a
ghost gets a fright?
He jumps into his skin.

What do you call a dinosaur with
a banana in each ear?
Anything you like. He can't hear you.

Henry's Halloween Howlers

Why didn't the witch
wear a flat cap?
There was no point.

Do zombies eat crisps
with their fingers?
No, they eat the
fingers separately.

What did the mother ghost say
to the naughty baby ghost?
*Don't spook until you're
spoken to.*

Why didn't the skeleton
go swimming?
*He had no body to
go with.*

HORRID HENRY AND THE DEMON DINNER LADY

'You're not having a packed lunch and that's final,' yelled Dad.

'It's not fair!' yelled Horrid Henry. 'Everyone in my class has a packed lunch.'

'N-O spells no,' said Dad. 'It's too much work. And you never eat what I pack for you.'

'But I hate school dinners!' screamed Henry. 'I'm being poisoned!' He clutched his throat. 'Dessert today was— bleeeach—fruit salad! And it had worms in it! I can feel them slithering in my stomach

21

– uggghh!' Horrid Henry fell to the floor, gasping and rasping.

Mum continued watching TV.

Dad continued watching TV.

'I love school dinners,' said Perfect Peter. 'They're so nutritious and delicious. Especially those lovely spinach salads.'

'Shut up, Peter!' snarled Henry.

'Muuuum!' wailed Peter. 'Henry told me to shut up!'

'Don't be horrid, Henry!' said Mum. 'You're not having a packed lunch and that's that.'

Horrid Henry and his parents had been fighting about packed lunches for weeks. Henry was desperate to have a packed lunch. Actually, he was desperate *not* to have a school dinner.

Horrid Henry hated school dinners. The stinky smell. The terrible way Sloppy Sally ladled the food *splat!* on his tray so that most of it splashed all over him. And the food! Queueing for hours for revolting ravioli and squashed tomatoes. The lumpy custard. The blobby mashed potatoes. Horrid Henry could not bear it any longer.

'Oh please,' said Henry. 'I'll make the packed lunch myself.' Wouldn't that be great! He'd fill his lunchbox with four packs of crisps, chocolate, doughnuts, cake, lollies, and one grape. Now that's what I call a real lunch, thought Henry.

Mum sighed.

Dad sighed.

They looked at each other.

'If you promise that everything in your lunchbox will get eaten, then I'll do a packed lunch for you,' said Dad.

'Oh thank you thank you thank you!' said Horrid Henry. 'Everything will get eaten, I promise.' Just not by me, he thought gleefully. Packed lunch room, here I come. Food fights, food swaps, food fun at last. Yippee!

Horrid Henry strolled into the packed lunch room. He was King Henry the

Horrible, surveying his unruly subjects. All around him children were screaming and shouting, pushing and shoving, throwing food and trading treats. Heaven! Horrid Henry smiled happily and opened his Terminator Gladiator lunchbox.

Hmmn. An egg salad sandwich. On brown bread. With crusts. Yuck! But he could always swap it for one of Greedy Graham's stack of chocolate spread sandwiches. Or one of Rude Ralph's jam rolls. That was the great thing about packed lunches, thought Henry. Someone always wanted what you had. No one *ever* wanted someone else's school dinner. Henry shuddered.

But those bad days were behind him, part of the dim and distant past. A horror story to tell his grandchildren. Henry could see it now. A row of horrified toddlers, screaming and crying while he told terrifying tales of stringy stew and soggy semolina.

Now, what else? Henry's fingers closed on something round. An apple. Great, thought Henry, he could use

it for target practice, and the carrots
would be perfect for poking Gorgeous
Gurinder when she wasn't looking.

Henry dug deeper. What was buried
right at the bottom? What was hidden
under the celery sticks and the granola
bar? Oh boy! Crisps! Henry loved crisps.
So salty! So crunchy! So yummy! His
mean, horrible parents only let him have
crisps once a week. Crisps! What bliss!
He could taste their delicious saltiness
already. He wouldn't share them with
anyone, no matter how hard they
begged. Henry tore open the bag and
reached in—

Suddenly a huge
shadow fell over him. A
fat greasy hand shot out.
Snatch! Crunch. Crunch.

Horrid Henry's crisps
were gone.

Henry was so shocked that for a moment he could not speak. 'Wha—wha—what was that?' gasped Henry as a gigantic woman waddled between the tables. 'She just stole my crisps!'

'That,' said Rude Ralph grimly, 'was Greta. 'She's the demon dinner lady.'

'Watch out for her!' squealed Sour Susan.

'She's the sneakiest snatcher in school,' wailed Weepy William.

What? A dinner lady who snatched food instead of dumping it on your plate? How could this be? Henry stared as Greasy Greta patrolled up and down the aisles. Her piggy eyes darted from side to side. She ignored Aerobic Al's carrots. She ignored Tidy Ted's yoghurt. She ignored Goody-Goody Gordon's orange.

Then suddenly—

Snatch! Chomp. Chomp.
Sour Susan's sweets were gone.
Snatch! Chomp. Chomp.
Dizzy Dave's doughnut

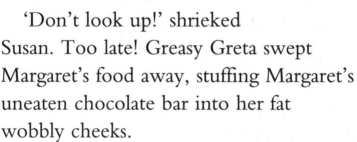

was gone.
Snatch! Chomp.
Chomp. Beefy Bert's
biscuits were gone.
Moody Margaret
looked up from
her lunch.

'Don't look up!' shrieked
Susan. Too late! Greasy Greta swept
Margaret's food away, stuffing Margaret's
uneaten chocolate bar into her fat
wobbly cheeks.

'Hey, I wasn't finished!' screamed
Margaret. Greasy Greta ignored her and
marched on. Weepy William tried to hide
his toffees under his cheese sandwich.
But Greasy Greta wasn't fooled.

Snatch! Gobble. Gobble. The toffees vanished down Greta's gaping gob.

'Waaah,' wailed William. 'I want my toffees!'

'No sweets in school,' barked Greasy
Greta. She marched up and down, up and
down, snatching and grabbing, looting
and devouring, wobbling and gobbling.

Why had no one told him there was
a demon dinner lady in charge of the
packed lunch room?

'Why didn't you warn me about her,
Ralph?' demanded Henry.

Rude Ralph shrugged. 'It wouldn't
have done any good. She is unstoppable.'

We'll see about that, thought Henry.
He glared at Greta. No way would
Greasy Greta grab his food again.

On Tuesday Greta snatched Henry's
doughnut.

On Wednesday Greta snatched
Henry's cake.

On Thursday Greta snatched Henry's
biscuits.

On Friday, as usual, Horrid Henry persuaded Anxious Andrew to swap his crisps for Henry's granola bar. He persuaded Kung-Fu Kate to swap her chocolates for Henry's raisins. He persuaded Beefy Bert to swap his biscuits for Henry's carrots. But what was the use of being a brilliant food trader, thought Henry miserably, if Greasy Greta just swooped and snaffled his hard-won treats?

Henry tried hiding his desserts. He tried eating his desserts secretly. He tried tugging them back. But it was no use.

The moment he snapped open his lunch box – SNATCH! Greasy Greta grabbed the goodies.

Something had to be done.

'Mum,' complained Henry, 'there's a demon dinner lady at school snatching our sweets.'

'That's nice, Henry,' said Mum, reading her newspaper.

'Dad,' complained Henry, 'there's a demon dinner lady at school snatching our sweets.'

'Good,' said Dad. 'You eat too many sweets.'

'We're not allowed to bring sweets to school, Henry,' said Perfect Peter.

'But it's not fair!' squealed Henry. 'She takes crisps, too.'

'If you don't like it, go back to school dinners,' said Dad.

'No!' howled Henry. 'I hate school
dinners!' Watery gravy with bits. Lumpy
surprise with lumps. Gristly glop
with globules. Food with its own life
slopping about on his tray. NO!

Horrid Henry couldn't face it. He'd
fought so hard for a packed lunch. Even
a packed lunch like the one Dad made,
fortified with eight essential minerals
and vitamins, was better than going back
to school dinners.

He could, of course, just eat healthy
foods. Greta never snatched those.
Henry imagined his lunchbox, groaning
with alfalfa sprouts on wholemeal brown
bread studded with chewy bits. Ugh!
Bleeeach! Torture!

He had to keep his packed lunch.
But he had to stop Greta. He just had to.

And then suddenly Henry had a brilliant, spectacular idea. It was so brilliant that for a moment he could hardly believe he'd thought of it. Oh boy, Greta, thought Henry gleefully, are you going to be sorry you messed with me.

Lunchtime. Horrid Henry sat with his lunchbox unopened. Rude Ralph was armed and ready beside him. Now, where was Greta?

Thump. Thump. Thump. The floor shook as the demon dinner lady started her food patrol. Horrid Henry waited

35

until she was almost behind him. SNAP!
He opened his lunchbox.

SNATCH! The familiar greasy hand
shot out, grabbed Henry's biscuits and
shovelled them into her mouth. Her
terrible teeth began to chomp.

And then—

'Yiaowwww! Aaaarrrgh!' A terrible
scream echoed through the packed
lunch room.

36

Greasy Greta turned purple. Then pink. Then bright red.

'Yiaowwww!' she howled. 'I need to cool down! Gimme that!' she screeched, snatching Rude Ralph's doughnut and stuffing it in her mouth.

'Aaaarrrgh!' she choked. 'I'm on fire! Water! Water!'

She grabbed a pitcher of water, poured it on top of herself, then ran howling down the aisle and out the door.

For a moment there was silence.
Then the entire packed lunch room
started clapping and cheering.

'Wow, Henry,' said Greedy Graham,
'what did you do to her?'

'Nothing,' said Horrid Henry. 'She
just tried my special recipe. Hot chilli
powder biscuits, anyone?'

Henry's Halloween Howlers

What kind of monster
has the best earing?
The eeriest.

What happens when a
ghost gets lost in the fog?
He is mist.

What do you get if you cross a
ghost with a packet of crisps?
Snacks that go crunch in the night.

What's the difference
between school dinners
and slugs?
*School dinners come
on plates.*

HORRID HENRY AND THE BOGEY BABYSITTER

'No way!' shrieked Tetchy Tess,
slamming down the phone.

'No way!' shrieked Crabby Chris,
slamming down the phone.

'No way!' shrieked Angry Anna.
'What do you think I am, crazy?'

Even Mellow Martin said he was busy.

Mum hung up the phone and groaned.

It wasn't easy finding someone to
babysit more than once for Horrid
Henry. When Tetchy Tess came, Henry
flooded the bathroom. When Crabby
Chris came he hid her homework and

'accidentally' poured red grape juice
down the front of her new white jeans.
And when Angry Anna came Henry –
no, it's too dreadful. Suffice it to say that
Anna ran screaming from the house and
Henry's parents had to come home early.

Horrid Henry hated babysitters. He
wasn't a baby. He didn't want to be sat
on. Why should he be nice to some ugly,
stuck-up, bossy teenager who'd hog the
TV and pig out on Henry's biscuits?
Parents should just stay at home where
they belonged, thought Horrid Henry.

And now it looked like they would
have to. Ha! His parents were mean and
horrible, but he'd had a lot of practice
managing them. Babysitters were unpre-
dictable. Babysitters were hard work.
And by the time you'd broken them in
and shown them who was boss, for some
reason they didn't want to come any more.

The only good babysitters let you stay up all night and eat sweets until you were sick. Sadly, Horrid Henry never got one of those.

'We have to find a babysitter,' wailed Mum. 'The party is tomorrow night. I've tried everyone. Who else is there?'

'There's got to be someone,' said Dad. 'Think!'

Mum thought.

Dad thought.

'What about Rebecca?' said Dad.

Horrid Henry's heart missed a beat. He stopped drawing moustaches on Perfect Peter's school pictures. Maybe

he'd heard wrong. Oh please, not
Rebecca! Not – Rabid Rebecca!

'Who did you say?' asked Henry.
His voice quavered.

'You heard me,' said Dad. 'Rebecca.'

'NO!' screamed Henry. 'She's horrible!'

'She's not horrible,' said Dad. 'She's
just – strict.'

'There's no one else,' said Mum
grimly. 'I'll phone Rebecca.'

'She's a monster!' wailed Henry. 'She
made Ralph go to bed at six o'clock!'

'I like going to bed at six o'clock,'
said Perfect Peter. 'After all, growing
children need their rest.'

Horrid Henry growled and attacked.

He was the Creature from the Black
Lagoon, dragging the foolish mortal down
to a watery grave.

'AAAEEEEE!' squealed Peter. 'Henry
pulled my hair.'

'Stop being horrid, Henry!' said Dad.
'Mum's on the phone.'

Henry prayed. Maybe she'd be busy.
Maybe she'd say no. Maybe she'd be
dead. He'd heard all about Rebecca.
She'd made Tough Toby get in his pyjamas
at five o'clock *and* do all his homework.
She'd unplugged Dizzy Dave's computer.

She'd made Moody Margaret wash the
floor. No doubt about it, Rabid Rebecca
was the toughest teen in town.

Henry lay on the rug and howled.
Mum shouted into the phone.

'You can! That's great, Rebecca. No,
that's just the TV – sorry for the noise.
See you tomorrow.'

'NOOOOOOOOO!' wailed Henry.

Ding dong.

'I'll get it!' said Perfect Peter. He
skipped to the door.

Henry flung himself on the carpet.

'I DON'T WANT TO HAVE A
BABYSITTER!' he wailed.

The door opened. In walked the
biggest, meanest, ugliest, nastiest-looking
girl Henry had ever seen. Her arms were
enormous. Her head was enormous.
Her teeth were enormous. She looked

47

like she ate elephants for breakfast, crocodiles for lunch, and snacked on toddlers for tea.

'What have you got to eat?' snarled Rabid Rebecca.

Dad took a step back. 'Help yourself to anything in the fridge,' said Dad.

'Don't worry, I will,' said Rebecca.

'GO HOME, YOU WITCH!' howled Henry.

'Bedtime is nine o'clock,' shouted Dad, trying to be heard above Henry's screams. He edged his way carefully past Rebecca, jumped over Henry, then dashed out the front door.

'I DON'T WANT TO HAVE A BABYSITTER!' shrieked Henry.

'Be good, Henry,' said Mum weakly.

48

She stepped over Henry, then escaped from the house.

The door closed.

Horrid Henry was alone in the house with Rabid Rebecca.

He glared at Rebecca.

Rebecca glared at him.

'I've heard all about you, you little creep,' growled Rebecca. 'No one bothers me when I'm babysitting.'

Horrid Henry stopped screaming.

'Oh yeah,' said Horrid Henry. 'We'll see about that.'

Rabid Rebecca bared her fangs. Henry recoiled. Perhaps I'd better keep out of her way, he thought, then slipped into the sitting room and turned on the telly.

Ahh, Mutant Max. Hurray! How bad could life be when a brilliant program like Mutant Max was on? He'd annoy Rebecca as soon as it was over.

Rebecca stomped into the room and snatched the clicker.

ZAP!

DA DOO, DA DOO DA, DA DOO DA DOO DA, tangoed some horrible spangly dancers.

'Hey,' said Henry. 'I'm watching Mutant Max.'

'Tough,' said Rebecca. '*I'm* watching ballroom dancing.'

Snatch!

Horrid Henry grabbed the clicker.

ZAP!

'And it's mutants, mutants, mut – '

Snatch!

Zap!

DA DOO, DA DOO DA, DA DOO
DA DOO DA.

DOO, DA DOO DA, DA DOO DA
DOO DA.

Horrid Henry tangoed round the room,
gliding and sliding.

'Stop it,' muttered Rebecca.

Henry shimmied back and forth in front
of the telly, blocking her view and singing
along as loudly as he could.

'DA DOO, DA DOO DA,' warbled
Henry.

'I'm warning you,' hissed Rebecca.

Perfect Peter walked in. He had already
put on his blue bunny pyjamas, brushed his
teeth and combed his hair. He held a game
of Chinese Checkers in his hand.

'Rebecca, will you play a game with me
before I go to bed?' asked Peter.

'NO!' roared Rebecca. 'I'm trying to
watch TV. Shut up and go away.'

Perfect Peter leapt back.

'But I thought – since I was all ready for bed – ' he stammered.

'I've got better things to do than to play with you,' snarled Rebecca. 'Now go to bed this minute, both of you.'

'But it's not my bedtime for hours,' protested Henry. 'I want to watch Mutant Max.'

'Nor mine,' said Perfect Peter timidly. 'There's this nature programme – '

'GO!' howled Rebecca.

'NO!' howled Henry.

'RAAAAA!' roared Rabid Rebecca.

Horrid Henry did not know how it happened. It was as if fiery dragon's breath had blasted him upstairs. Somehow, he was in his pyjamas, in

54

bed, and it was only seven o'clock.

Rabid Rebecca switched off the light.

'Don't even think of moving from that bed,' she hissed. 'If I see you, or hear you, or even smell you, you'll be sorry you were born. I'll stay downstairs, you stay upstairs, and that way no one will get hurt.' Then she marched out of the room and slammed the door.

Horrid Henry was so shocked he could not move. He, Horrid Henry, the bulldozer of babysitters, the terror of teachers, the bully of brothers, was in bed, lights out, at seven o'clock.

Seven o'clock! Two whole hours before his bedtime! This was an outrage! He could hear Moody Margaret shrieking next door. He could hear

55

Toddler Tom zooming about on his tricycle. No one went to bed at seven o'clock. Not even toddlers!

Worst of all, he was thirsty. So what if she told me to stay in bed, thought Horrid Henry. I'm thirsty. I'm going to go downstairs and get myself a glass of water. It's my house and I'll do what I want.

Horrid Henry did not move.

I'm dying of thirst here, thought Henry. Mum and Dad will come home and

I'll be a dried out old stick insect, and boy will she be in trouble.

Horrid Henry still did not move.

Go on, feet, urged Henry, let's just step on down and get a little ol' glass of water. So what if that bogey babysitter said he had to stay in bed. What could she do to him?

She could chop off my head and bounce it down the stairs, thought Henry.

Eeek.

Well, let her try.

Horrid Henry remembered who he was. The boy who'd sent teachers shrieking from the classroom. The boy who'd destroyed the Demon Dinner Lady. The boy who had run away from home and almost reached the Congo.

57

I will get up and get a drink of water, he thought.

Sneak. Sneak. Sneak.

Horrid Henry crept to the bedroom door.

Slowly he opened it a crack.

Creak.

Then slowly, slowly, he opened the door a bit more and slipped out.

ARGHHHHHH!

There was Rabid Rebecca sitting at the top of the stairs.

It's a trap, thought Henry. She was lying in wait for me. I'm dead, I'm finished, they'll find my bones in the morning.

Horrid Henry dashed back inside his room and awaited his doom.

Silence.

What was going on? Why hadn't

Rebecca torn him apart limb from limb?

Horrid Henry opened his door a fraction and peeped out.

Rabid Rebecca was still sitting huddled at the top of the stairs. She did not move. Her eyes were fixed straight ahead.

'Spi–spi–spider,' she whispered. She pointed at a big, hairy spider in front of her with a trembling hand.

'It's huge,' said Henry. 'Really hairy and horrible and wriggly and— '

'STOP!' squealed Rebecca. 'Help me, Henry,' she begged.

Horrid Henry was not the fearless leader of a pirate gang for nothing.

'If I risk my life and get rid of the

spider, can I watch Mutant Max?' said
Henry.

'Yes,' said Rebecca.

'And stay up 'til my parents come home?'

'Yes,' said Rebecca.

'And eat all the ice cream in the fridge?'

'YES!' shrieked Rebecca. 'Just get rid
of that – that – '

'Deal,' said Horrid Henry.

He dashed to his room and grabbed
a jar.

Rabid Rebecca hid her eyes as Horrid
Henry scooped up the spider. What a
beauty!

'It's gone,' said Henry.

Rebecca opened her beady red eyes.

'Right, back to bed, you little brat!'

'What?' said Henry.

'Bed. Now!' screeched Rebecca.

'But we agreed . . .' said Henry.

'Tough,' said Rebecca. 'That was then.'

'Traitor,' said Henry.

He whipped out the spider jar from behind his back and unscrewed the lid.

'On guard!' he said.

'AAEEEE!' whimpered Rebecca.

Horrid Henry advanced menacingly towards her.

'NOOOOOOO!' wailed Rebecca, stepping back.

'Now get in that room and stay there,' ordered Henry. 'Or else.'

Rabid Rebecca skedaddled into the bathroom and locked the door.

'If I see you or hear you or even smell you you'll be sorry you were born,' said Henry.

'I already am,' said Rabid Rebecca.

Horrid Henry spent a lovely evening in front of the telly. He watched scary movies. He ate ice cream and sweets and biscuits and crisps until he could stuff no more in.

Vroom vroom.

Oops. Parents home.

Horrid Henry dashed upstairs and leapt into bed just as the front door opened.

Mum and Dad looked around the sitting room, littered with sweet wrappers, biscuit crumbs and ice cream cartons.

'You did tell her to help herself,' said Mum.

'Still,' said Dad. 'What a pig.'

'Never mind,' said Mum brightly, 'at least she managed to get Henry to bed.

That's a first.'

Rabid Rebecca staggered into the room.

'Did you get enough to eat?' said Dad.

'No,' said Rabid Rebecca.

'Oh,' said Dad.

'Was everything all right?' asked Mum.

Rebecca looked at her.

'Can I go now?' said Rebecca.

'Any chance you could babysit on Saturday?' asked Dad hopefully.

'What do you think I am, crazy?' shrieked Rebecca.

SLAM!

Upstairs, Horrid Henry groaned.

Rats. It was so unfair. Just when he had a babysitter beautifully trained, for some reason they wouldn't come back.

Henry's Halloween Howlers

Did you hear about the
vampire who needed a drink?
He was bloodthirsty.

What do you get if you cross
a ghost with a footballer?
A ghoulie.

How do monsters cook
their food?
They terror-fry it.

What goes ha-ha-bonk?
A man laughing his head off.

Henry's Halloween Howlers

What's the scariest
squidgiest day of the year?
Marshalloween.

What does an alien from
Mars like to eat?
Martian-mellows.

What monster do you get
at the end of your finger?
A bogey monster.

Why did the mummy
have no friends?
*He was too wrapped
up in himself.*

MOODY MARGARET CASTS A SPELL

'You are getting sleepy,' said Moody Margaret. 'You are getting very sleepy . . . '

Slowly she waved her watch in front of Susan.

'So sleepy . . . you are now asleep . . . you are now fast asleep . . . '

'No I'm not,' said Sour Susan.

'When I click my fingers you will start snoring.'

Margaret clicked her fingers.

'But I'm not asleep,' said Susan.

Margaret glared at her.

'How am I supposed to hypnotise you if you don't try?' said Margaret.

'I *am* trying, you're just a bad hypnotist,'

said Susan sourly. 'Now it's my turn.'

'No it's not, it's still mine,' said Margaret.

'You've had your go,' said Susan.

'No I haven't!'

'But I never get to be the hypnotist!' wailed Susan.

'Cry baby!'

'Meanie!'

'Cheater!'

'Cheater!'

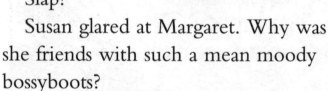

Slap!

Slap!

Susan glared at Margaret. Why was she friends with such a mean moody bossyboots?

Margaret glared at Susan. Why was she friends with such a stupid sour sulker?

'I hate you, Margaret!' screamed Sour Susan.

'I hate you more!' screamed Moody Margaret.

'Shut up, landlubbers!' shrieked Horrid Henry from his hammock in the garden next door. 'Or the Purple Hand will make you walk the plank!'

'Shut up yourself, Henry,' said Margaret.

'Yeah, Henry,' said Susan.

'You are stupid, you are stupid,' chanted Rude Ralph, who was playing pirates with Henry.

'You're the stupids,' snapped Moody Margaret. 'Now leave us alone, we're busy.'

'Henry, can I play pirates with you?' asked Perfect Peter, wandering out from the house.

'No, you puny prawn!' screamed Captain Hook. 'Out of my way before I tear you to pieces with my hook!'

'Muuum,' wailed Peter. 'Henry said he was going to tear me to pieces!'

'Stop being horrid, Henry!' shouted Mum.

'And he won't let me play with him,' said Peter.

'Can't you be nice to your brother for once?' said Dad.

NO! thought Horrid Henry. Why should he be nice to that tell-tale brat? Horrid Henry did not want to play pirates with Peter. Peter was the world's worst pirate. He couldn't swordfight. He couldn't swashbuckle. He couldn't remember pirate curses. All he could do was whine.

'Okay, Peter, you're the prisoner. Wait in the fort,' said Henry.

'But I'm always the prisoner,' said Peter. Henry glared at him.

'Do you want to play or don't you?'

'Yes Captain,' said Peter. He crawled into the lair of the Purple Hand. Being prisoner was better than nothing, he supposed. He just hoped he wouldn't have to wait too long.

'Let's get out of here quick,' Henry whispered to Rude Ralph. 'I've got a great idea for playing a trick on Margaret and Susan.' He whispered to Ralph. Ralph grinned.

Horrid Henry hoisted himself onto the low brick wall between his garden and Margaret's.

Moody Margaret was still waving her watch at Susan. Unfortunately, Susan had her back turned and her arms folded.

'Go away, Henry,' ordered Margaret.

'Yeah Henry,' said Susan. 'No boys.'

'Are you being hypnotists?' said Henry.

'Margaret's trying to hypnotise me, only she can't 'cause she's a rubbish hypnotist,' said Susan.

'That's your fault,' said Margaret, glaring.

'Of course you can't hypnotise her,' said Henry. 'You're doing it all wrong.'

74

'And what would you know about that?' asked Margaret.

'Because,' said Horrid Henry, 'I am a master hypnotist.'

Moody Margaret laughed.

'He is too a master hypnotist,' said Ralph. 'He hypnotises me all the time.'

'Oh yeah?' said Margaret.

'Yeah,' said Henry.

'Prove it,' said Margaret.

'Okay,' said Horrid Henry. 'Gimme the watch.'

Margaret handed it over.

He turned to Ralph.

'Look into my eyes,' he ordered.

Ralph looked into Henry's eyes.

'Now watch the watch,' ordered Henry the hypnotist, swinging the watch back and forth. Rude Ralph swayed.

'You will obey my commands,' said Henry.

'I – will – obey,' said Ralph in a
robot voice.

'When I whistle, you will jump off
the wall,' said Henry. He whistled.

Ralph jumped off the wall.

'See?' said Horrid Henry.

'That doesn't prove he's hypnotised,'
said Margaret. 'You have to make him
do silly things.'

'Like what?' said Henry.

'Tell him he's got no clothes on.'

'Ralph, you're a
nudie,' said Henry.

Ralph immediately
started running round
the garden shrieking.

'Aaaaaaarrgghh!'
yelped Ralph. 'I'm a
nudie! I'm a nudie!
Give me some clothes, help help! No
one look, I'm naked!'

Margaret hesitated. There was no way Henry could have *really* hypnotised Ralph – was there?

'I still don't believe he's hypnotised,' said Margaret.

'Then watch this,' said Horrid Henry. 'Ralph – when I snap my fingers you will be . . . Margaret.'

Snap!

'My name is Margaret,' said Ralph. 'I'm a mean bossyboots. I'm the biggest bossiest boot. I'm a frogface.'

Margaret blushed red.

Susan giggled.

'It's not funny,' snapped Margaret. *No one* made fun of her and lived to tell the tale.

'See?' said Henry. 'He obeys my every command.'

'Wow,' said Susan. 'You really are a hypnotist. Can you teach me?'

'Maybe,' said Horrid Henry. 'How much will you pay me?'

'He's just a big faker,' said Margaret. She stuck her nose in the air. 'If you're such a great hypnotist, then hypnotise *me*.'

Oops. Now he was trapped. Margaret was trying to spoil his trick. Well, no way would he let her.

Horrid Henry remembered who he was. The boy who got Miss Battle-Axe sent to the head. The boy who terrified the bogey babysitter. The boy who tricked the Tooth Fairy. He could hypnotise Margaret any day.

'Sure,' he said, waving the watch in front of Margaret.

'You are getting sleepy,' droned Henry. 'You are getting very sleepy.

When I snap my fingers you will obey my every command.'

Henry snapped his fingers. Margaret glared at him.

'Well?' said Moody Margaret.

'Don't you know *anything*?' said Horrid Henry. He thought fast. 'That was just the beginning bit. I will complete part two once I have freed Ralph from my power. Ralph, repeat after me, "I am sellotape".'

'I am sellotape,' said Rude Ralph. Then he belched.

'I am burping sellotape,' said Rude Ralph. He caught Henry's eye. They burst out laughing.

'Ha ha, Susan, fooled you!' shrieked Henry.

'Did not,' shrieked Susan.

'Did too. Nah nah ne nah nah!' Henry and Ralph ran round Margaret, whooping and cheering.

'Come on Margaret,' said Susan.
'Let's go do some *real* hypnosis.'

Margaret didn't move.

'Come on, Margaret,' said Susan.

'I am sellotape,' said Margaret.

'No you're not,' said Susan.

'Yes I am,' said Margaret.

Henry and Ralph stopped whooping.

'There's something wrong with
Margaret,' said Susan. 'She's acting
all funny. Margaret, are you okay?
Margaret? Margaret?'

Moody Margaret stood very still. Her
eyes looked blank.

Horrid Henry snapped
his fingers.

'Raise your right arm,'
he ordered.

Margaret raised her
right arm.

80

Huh? thought Horrid Henry.

'Pinch Susan.'

Margaret pinched Susan.

'Owww!' yelped Susan.

'Repeat after me, "I am a stupid girl".'

'I am a stupid girl,' said Margaret.

'No you're not,' said Susan.

'Yes I am,' said Margaret.

'She's hypnotised,' said Horrid Henry. He'd actually hypnotised Moody Margaret. This was amazing. This was fantastic. He really truly was a master hypnotist!

'Will you obey me, slave?'

'I will obey,' said Margaret.

'When I click my fingers, you will be a . . . chicken.'

Click!

'Squawk! Squawk! Squawk!' cackled Margaret, flapping her arms wildly.

'What have you done to her?' wailed Sour Susan.

'Wow,' said Rude Ralph. 'You've hypnotised her.'

Horrid Henry could not believe his luck. If he could hypnotise Margaret, he could hypnotise anyone. Everyone would have to obey his commands. He would be master of the world! The universe! Everything!

Henry could see it now.

'Henry, ten out of ten,' Miss Battle-Axe would say. 'Henry is so clever he doesn't ever need to do homework again.'

Oh boy, would he fix Miss Battle-Axe.

He'd make her do the hula in a grass skirt when she wasn't running round the playground mooing like a cow.

He'd make the head Mrs Oddbod just have chocolate

and cake for school dinners. And no P.E.
– ever. In fact, he'd make Mrs Oddbod
close down the school.

And as for Mum and Dad . . .

'Henry, have as many sweets as you
like,' Dad would say.

'No bedtime for you,' Mum would say.

'Henry, watch as much TV as you
want,' Dad would say.

'Henry, here's your pocket money –
£1,000 a week. Tell us if you need more,'
Mum would smile.

'Peter, go to your room and stay there for a year!' Mum and Dad would scream.

Henry would hypnotise them all later. But first, what should he make Margaret do?

Ah yes. Her house was filled with sweets and biscuits and fizzy drinks – all the things Henry's horrible parents never let him have.

'Bring us all your sweets, all your biscuits and a Fizzywizz drink.'

'Yes, master,' said Moody Margaret.

Henry stretched out in the hammock. So did Rude Ralph. This was the life!

Sour Susan didn't know what to do. On the one hand, Margaret was mean and horrible, and she hated her. It was fun watching her obey orders for once. On the other hand, Susan would much rather Margaret was *her* slave than Henry's.

'Unhypnotise her, Henry,' said Sour Susan.

'Soon,' said Horrid Henry.

'Let's hypnotise Peter next,' said Ralph.

'Yeah,' said Henry. No more telling tales. No more goody goody vegetable-eating I'm Mr Perfect. Oh boy would he hypnotise Peter!

Moody Margaret came slowly out of her house. She was carrying a large pitcher and a huge bowl of chocolate mousse.

'Here is your Fizzywizz drink, master,' said Margaret. Then she poured it on top of him.

'Wha? Wha?' spluttered Henry, gasping and choking.

'And your dinner, frogface,' she added, tipping the mousse all over Ralph.

'Ugggh!' wailed Ralph.

'NAH NAH NE NAH NAH,'

shrieked Margaret. 'Fooled you! Fooled you!'

Perfect Peter crept out of the Purple-Hand Fort. What was all that yelling? It must be a pirate mutiny!

'Hang on pirates, here I come!' shrieked Peter, charging at the thrashing hammock as fast as he could.

CRASH!

A sopping wet pirate captain and a mousse-covered first mate lay on the ground. They stared up at their prisoner.

'Hi Henry,' said Peter. 'I mean, hi Captain.' He took a step backwards. 'I mean, Lord High Excellent Majesty.' He took another step back.

'Ugh, we were playing pirate mutiny – weren't we?'

'DIE, WORM!' yelled Horrid Henry, leaping up.

'MUUUUUUM!' shrieked Peter.

Henry's Halloween Howlers

Why do vampires like thick books?
They like stories they can really get their teeth into.

What's a baby ghost's favourite game?
Peek-A-BOO!

How do you join the Dracula fan club?
Send your name, address and blood group.

What do monsters like best for pudding?
Eyes-cream.

Henry's Halloween Howlers

What was the scariest
prehistoric animal?
The Terror-dactyl.

What's a vampire's favourite
kind of ice cream?
Vein-illa.

What kind of make-up do
witches wear?
Mas-scare-a.

What do short-sighted
ghosts wear?
Spooktacles.

HORRID HENRY
AND THE
FANGMANGLER

Horrid Henry snatched his skeleton
bank and tried to twist open the trap
door. Mum was taking him to Toy
Heaven tomorrow. At last Henry
would be able to buy the toy of his
dreams: a Dungeon Drink kit. Ha ha
ha – the tricks he'd play on his
family, substituting their drinks for
Dungeon stinkers.

Best of all, Moody Margaret would
be green with envy. She wanted a
Dungeon Drink kit too, but she

didn't have any money. He'd have one first, and no way was Margaret ever going to play with it. Except for buying the occasional sweet and a few comics, Henry had been saving his money for weeks.

Perfect Peter peeked round the door.

'I've saved £7.53,' said Peter proudly, jingling his piggy bank. 'More than enough to buy my nature kit. How much do you have?'

'Millions,' said Henry.

Perfect Peter gasped.

'You do not,' said Peter. 'Do you?'

Henry shook his bank. A thin rattle came from within.

'That doesn't sound like millions,' said Peter.

'That's 'cause five pound notes don't rattle, stupid,' said Henry.

'Mum! Henry called me stupid,' shrieked Peter.

'Stop being horrid, Henry!' shouted Mum.

Horrid Henry gave the lid of his bank a final yank and spilled the contents on to the floor.

A single, solitary five pence coin rolled out.

Henry's jaw dropped. He grabbed the bank and fumbled around inside. It was empty.

'I've been robbed!' howled Horrid Henry. 'Where's my money? Who stole my money?'

Mum ran into the room.

'What's all this fuss?'

'Peter stole my money!' screamed Henry. He glared at his brother. 'Just wait until I get my hands on you, you little thief, I'll –'

'No one stole your money, Henry,' said Mum. 'You've spent it all on sweets and comics.'

'I have not!' shrieked Henry.

Mum pointed at the enormous pile of comics and sweet wrappers littering the floor of Henry's bedroom.

'What's all that then?' asked Mum.

Horrid Henry stopped shrieking. It was true. He *had* spent all his pocket money on comics and sweets. He just hadn't noticed.

'It's not fair!' he screamed.

'I saved all *my* pocket money, Mum,' said Perfect Peter. 'After all, a penny saved is a penny earned.'

Mum smiled at him. 'Well done, Peter. Henry, let this be a lesson to you.'

'I can't wait to buy my nature kit,' said Perfect Peter. 'You should have saved your money like I did, instead of wasting it, Henry.'

Henry growled and sprang at Peter. He was an Indian warrior scalping a settler.

'YOWWWW!' squealed Peter.

'Henry! Stop it!' shouted Mum. 'Say sorry to Peter.'

'I'm not sorry!' screamed Henry. 'I want my money!'

'Any more nonsense from you,
young man, and we won't be going
to Toy Heaven,' said Mum.

Henry scowled.

'I don't care,' he muttered. What
was the point of going to Toy
Heaven if he couldn't buy any toys?

Horrid Henry lay on his bedroom floor kicking sweet wrappers. That Dungeon Drink kit cost £4.99. He had to get some money by tomorrow. The question was, how?

He could steal Peter's money. That was tempting, as he knew the secret place in Peter's cello case where Peter hid his bank. Wouldn't that be fun when Peter discovered his money was gone? Henry smiled.

On second thought, perhaps not. Mum and Dad would be sure to suspect Henry, especially if he suddenly had money and Peter didn't.

He could sell some of his comics to Moody Margaret.

'No!' shrieked Henry, clutching his comics to his chest. Not his precious comics. There *had* to be another way.

Then Henry had a wonderful, spectacular idea. It was so superb that he did a wild war dance for joy. That Dungeon Drink kit was as good as his. And, better still, Peter would give him all the money he needed. Henry chortled. This would be as easy as taking sweets from a baby . . . and a lot more fun.

Horrid Henry strolled down the hall to Peter's room. Peter was having a meeting of the Best Boys Club (motto: Can I help?) with his friends Tidy Ted, Spotless Sam and Goody-Goody Gordon. What luck. More money for him. Henry smiled as he put his ear to the keyhole and listened to them discussing their good deeds.

'I helped an old lady cross the road

and I ate all my vegetables,' said Perfect Peter.

'I kept my room tidy all week,' said Tidy Ted.

'I scrubbed the bath without being asked,' said Spotless Sam.

'I never once forgot to say please and thank you,' said Goody-Goody Gordon.

Henry pushed past the barricades and burst into Peter's room.

'Password!' screeched Perfect Peter.

'Vitamins,' said Horrid Henry.

'How did you know?' said Tidy Ted, staring open-mouthed at Henry.

'Never you mind,' said Henry, who was not a master spy for nothing. 'I don't suppose any of you know about Fangmanglers?'

The boys looked at one another.

'What are they?' asked Spotless
Sam.

'Only the slimiest, scariest, most
horrible and frightening monsters in
the whole world,' said Henry. 'And
I know where to find one.'

'Where?' said Goody-Goody
Gordon.

'I'm not going to tell you,' said
Horrid Henry.

'Oh please!' said Spotless Sam.

Henry shook his head and lowered
his voice.

'Fangmanglers only come out at
night,' whispered Henry. 'They slip
into the shadows then sneak out and
. . . BITE YOU!' he suddenly
shrieked.

The Best Boys Club members
gasped with fright.

'I'm not scared,' said Peter. 'And
I've never heard of a Fangmangler.'

'That's because you're too
young,' said Henry. 'Grown-ups
don't tell you about them because
they don't want to scare you.'

'I want to see it,' said Tidy Ted.

'Me too,' said Spotless Sam and Goody-Goody Gordon.

Peter hesitated for a moment.

'Is this a trick, Henry?'

'Of course not,' said Henry. 'And just for that I won't let you come.'

'Oh please, Henry,' said Peter.

Henry paused.

'All right,' he said. 'We'll meet in the back garden after dark. But it will cost you two pounds each.'

'Two pounds!' they squealed.

'Do you want to see a Fangmangler or don't you?'

Perfect Peter exchanged a look with his friends.

They all nodded.

'Good,' said Horrid Henry. 'See you at six o'clock. And don't forget to bring your money.'

Tee hee, chortled Henry silently.

Eight pounds! He could get a Dungeon Drink kit *and* a Grisly Ghoul Grub box at this rate.

Loud screams came from next-door's garden.

'Give me back my spade!' came Moody Margaret's bossy tones.

'You're so mean, Margaret,' squealed Sour Susan's sulky voice. 'Well, I won't. It's my turn to dig with it now.'

WHACK! THWACK!

'WAAAAAAA!'

Eight pounds is nice, thought Horrid Henry, but twelve is even nicer.

'What's going on?' asked Horrid Henry, smirking as he leapt over the wall.

'Go away, Henry!' shouted Moody Margaret.

'Yeah, Henry,' echoed Sour
Susan, wiping away her tears. 'We
don't want you.'

'All right,' said Henry. 'Then I
won't tell you about the Fangmangler
I've found.'

'We don't want to know about it,'
said Margaret, turning her back on
him.

'That's right,' said Susan.

'Well then, don't blame me when the Fangmangler sneaks over the wall and rips you to pieces and chews up your guts,' said Horrid Henry. He turned to go.

The girls looked at one another.

'Wait,' ordered Margaret.

'Yeah?' said Henry.

'You don't scare me,' said Margaret.

'Prove it then,' said Henry.

'How?' said Margaret.

'Be in my garden at six o'clock tonight and I'll show you the Fangmangler. But it will cost you two pounds each.'

'Forget it,' said Margaret. 'Come on, Susan.'

'Okay,' said Henry quickly. 'One pound each.'

'No,' said Margaret.

'And your money back if the Fangmangler doesn't scare you,' said Henry.

Moody Margaret smiled.

'It's a deal,' she said.

When the coast was clear, Horrid Henry crept into the bushes and hid a bag containing his supplies: an old, torn T-shirt, some filthy trousers and

a jumbo-sized bottle of ketchup.
Then he sneaked back into the house
and waited for dark.

'Thank you, thank you, thank you,
thank you,' said Horrid Henry,
collecting two pounds from each
member of the Best Boys Club.
Henry placed the money carefully in
his skeleton bank. Boy, was he rich!

Moody Margaret and Sour Susan
handed over one pound each.

'Remember Henry, we get our
money back if we aren't scared,'
hissed Moody Margaret.

'Shut up, Margaret,' said Henry.
'I'm risking my life and all you can
think about is money. Now
everyone, wait here, don't move and
don't talk,' he whispered. 'We have
to surprise the Fangmangler. If

108

not . . .' Henry paused and drew his fingers across his throat. 'I'm a goner. I'm going off now to hunt for the monster. When I find him, and if it's safe, I'll whistle twice. Then everyone come, as quietly as you can. But be careful!'

Henry disappeared into the black darkness of the garden.

For a long long moment there was silence.

'This is stupid,' said Moody Margaret.

Suddenly, a low, moaning growl echoed through the moonless night.

'What was that?' said Spotless Sam nervously.

'Henry? Are you all right, Henry?' squeaked Perfect Peter.

The low moaning growl turned into a snarl.

THRASH! CRASH!

'HELP! HELP! THE FANGMANGLER'S AFTER ME! RUN FOR YOUR LIVES!' screamed Horrid Henry, smashing through the bushes. His T-shirt and trousers were torn. There was blood everywhere.

The Best Boys Club screamed and ran.

Sour Susan screamed and ran.

Moody Margaret screamed and ran.

Horrid Henry screamed and . . . stopped.

He waited until he was alone. Then

Horrid Henry wiped some ketchup
from his face, clutched his bank and
did a war dance round the garden,
whooping with joy.

'Money! Money! Money! Money!
Money!' he squealed, leaping and
stomping. He danced and he pranced,
he twirled and he whirled. He was so
busy dancing and cackling he didn't
notice a shadowy shape slip into the
garden behind him.

'Money! Money! Money! Mine!
Mine —' he broke off. What was that
noise? Horrid Henry's throat
tightened.

'Nah,' he thought. 'It's nothing.'

Then suddenly a dark shape leapt out of the bushes and let out a thunderous roar.

Horrid Henry shrieked with terror. He dropped his money and ran for his life. The Thing scooped up his bank and slithered over the wall.

Horrid Henry did not stop running until he was safely in his room with the door shut tight and barricaded. His heart pounded.

There really is a Fangmangler, he thought, trembling. And now it's after *me*.

Horrid Henry hardly slept a wink. He started awake at every squeak and creak. He shook and he shrieked. Henry had such a bad night that he slept in quite late the next morning, tossing and turning.

★

FIZZ! POP! GURGLE! BANG!

Henry jerked awake. What was that? He peeked his head out from under the duvet and listened.

FIZZ! POP! GURGLE! BANG!

Those fizzing and popping noises seemed to be coming from next door.

Henry ran to the window and pulled open the curtains. There was Moody Margaret sitting beside a large Toy Heaven bag. In front of her was . . . a Dungeon Drink kit. She saw him, smiled, and raised a glass of bubbling black liquid.

'Want a Fangmangler drink, Henry?' asked Margaret sweetly.

Henry's Halloween Howlers

What do you call a witch's garage?
A broom cupboard.

What lies on the ground, a
hundred feet in the air?
A centipede.

How do monsters count
to twenty-three?
On their fingers.

What do you get when
you cross a cow with a
werewolf?
A burger that bites back.

Snash!
Snash!

Henry's Halloween Howlers

DIZZY DAVE: My bike's haunted.
HORRID HENRY: How do you know?
DIZZY DAVE: Because it's got
spooks on the wheels.

What pets does
Dracula own?
*A bloodhound and
a ghoulfish.*

What do you call a
monster with no neck?
The Lost Neck Monster.

What is green and
eats porridge?
Mouldy Locks.

HORRID HENRY'S MONSTER MOVIE

Horrid Henry loved scary movies. He loved nothing more than curling up on the comfy black chair with a huge bag of popcorn and a Fizzywizz drink, and jumping out of his seat in shock every few minutes. He loved wailing ghosts, oozing swamps, and bloodthirsty monsters. No film was too scary or too creepy for Horrid Henry. MWAHAHAHAHAHAHA!

Perfect Peter hated scary movies. He hated nothing more than hiding behind the comfy black chair covering his eyes and jumping out of his skin in shock every few seconds. He hated ghosts and swamps and monsters. Even Santa Claus saying 'ho ho ho' too loudly scared him.

Thanks to Peter being the biggest scaredy-cat who ever lived, Mum and Dad would never take Henry to see any scary films.

And now, the scariest, most frightening, most terrible film ever was in town. Horrid Henry was desperate to see it.

'You're not seeing that film and that's final,' said Mum.

'Absolutely no way,' said Dad. 'Far too scary.'

'But I love scary movies!' shrieked Horrid Henry.

'I don't,' said Mum.

'I don't,' said Dad.

'I hate scary movies,' said Perfect Peter.

'Please can we see *The Big Bunny Caper* instead?'

'NO!' shrieked Horrid Henry.

'Stop shouting, Henry,' said Mum.

'But everyone's seen *The Vampire Zombie Werewolf*,' moaned Horrid Henry. 'Everyone but me.'

Moody Margaret had seen it, and said it was the best horror film ever.

Fiery Fiona had seen it three times. 'And I'm seeing it three more times,' she squealed.

Rude Ralph said he'd run screaming from the cinema.

AAAARRRRGGGGHHHHHH.

Horrid Henry thought he would explode he wanted to see *The Vampire Zombie Werewolf* so much. But no. The film came and went, and Horrid Henry wailed and gnashed.

So he couldn't believe his luck when Rude Ralph came up to him one day at playtime and said:

'I've got *The Vampire Zombie Werewolf* film on DVD. Want to come over and watch it after school?'

Did he ever!

★

Horrid Henry squeezed onto the sofa between Rude Ralph and Brainy Brian. Dizzy Dave sat on the floor next to Jolly Josh and Aerobic Al. Anxious Andrew sat on a chair. He'd already covered his face with his hands. Even Moody Margaret and Sour Susan were there, squabbling over who got to sit in the armchair and who had to sit on the floor.

'OK everyone, this is it,' said Rude Ralph. 'The scariest film ever. Are we ready?'

'Yeah!'

Horrid Henry gripped the sofa as the eerie piano music started.

There was a deep, dark forest.

'I'm scared!' wailed Anxious Andrew.

'Nothing's happened yet,' said Horrid Henry.

A boy and a girl ran through the shivery, shadowy trees.

'Is it safe to look?' gasped Anxious Andrew.

'Shhh,' said Moody Margaret.

'You shhh!' said Horrid Henry.

'MWAHAAAAHAAAAHAHAHAA!' bellowed Dizzy Dave.

'I'm scared!' shrieked Anxious Andrew.

'Shut up!' shouted Rude Ralph.

The pale girl stopped running and turned to the bandaged boy.

'I can't kiss you or I'll turn into a zombie,' sulked the girl.

'I can't kiss *you* or *I'll* turn into a vampire,' scowled the boy.

'But our love is so strong!' wailed the vampire girl and the zombie boy.

'Not as strong as me!' howled the werewolf, leaping out from behind a tree stump.

'AAAAAAAARRRRGGGHHH!' screeched Anxious Andrew.

'SHUT UP!' shouted Henry and Ralph.

'Leave her alone, you walking bandage,' said the werewolf.

'Leave him alone, you smelly fur ball,' said the vampire.

'This isn't scary,' said Horrid Henry.

'Shh,' said Margaret.

'Go away!' shouted the zombie.

'You go away, you big meanie,' snarled the werewolf.

'Don't you know that two's company and three's a crowd?' hissed the vampire.

'I challenge you both to an arm-wrestling contest,' howled the werewolf. 'The winner gets to keep the arms.'

'Or in your case the paws,' sniffed the vampire.

'This is the worst film I've ever seen,' said Horrid Henry.

'Shut up, Henry,' said Margaret.

'We're trying to watch,' said Susan.

'Ralph, I thought you said this was a really scary film,' hissed Henry. 'Have you *actually* seen it before?'

Rude Ralph looked at the floor.

'No,' admitted Ralph. 'But everyone said they'd seen it and I didn't want to be left out.'

'Margaret's a big fat liar too,' said Susan. 'She never saw it either.'

'Shut up, Susan!' shrieked Margaret.

'Awhooooooo,' howled the werewolf.

Horrid Henry was disgusted. He could make a *much* scarier film. In fact . . . what was stopping him? Who better to make the scariest film of all time than

Henry? How hard could it be to make
a film? You just pointed a camera and
yelled, 'Action!' Then he'd be rich rich
rich. He'd need a spare house just to
stash all his cash. And he'd be famous,
too. Everyone would be begging
for a role in one of his mega-horror
blockbusters. "Please can we be in your
new monster film?" Mum and Dad and
Peter would beg. Well, they could beg
as long as they liked. He'd give them his
autograph, but that would be *it*.

Henry could see the poster now:

```
HENRY PRODUCTIONS
PRESENT:

THE UNDEAD
DEMON MONSTER
WHO WOULD
NOT DIE

Starring HENRY as The Monster

Written and Filmed and Directed by
HENRY
```

'I could make a *really* scary film,' said
Henry.

'Not as scary as the film *I* could
make,' said Margaret.

'Ha!' said Henry. 'Your scary film wouldn't scare a toddler.'

'Ha!' said Margaret. '*Your* scary film would make a baby laugh.'

'Oh yeah?' said Henry.

'Yeah,' said Margaret.

'Well, we'll just see about that,' said Henry.

Horrid Henry walked around his garden, clutching Mum's camcorder. He could turn the garden into a swamp . . . flood a few flower beds . . . rip up the lawn and throw buckets of mud at the windows as the monster squelched his monstrous way through the undergrowth, growling and devouring, biting and—

'Henry, can I be in your movie?' said Peter.

'No,' said Henry. 'I'm making a scary

monster film. No nappy babies.'

'I am not a nappy baby,' said Peter.

'Are too.'

'Am not. Mum! Henry won't let me be in his film.'

'Henry!' yelled Mum. 'Let Peter be in your film or you can't borrow the camcorder.'

Gah! Why did everyone always get in his way? How could Henry be a

great director if other people told him
who to put in his film?

'Okay Peter,' said Henry, scowling.
'You can be Best Boy.'

Best Boy! That sounded super. Wow.
That was a lot better than Peter had
hoped.

'Best Boy!' shouted Horrid Henry.
'Get the snack table ready.'

'*Snack* table?' said Peter.

'Setting up the snack table is the most
important part of making a movie,' said
Henry. 'So I want biscuits and crisps and

Fizzywizz drinks – NOW!' he bellowed. 'It's hungry work making a film.'

Film-making next door at Moody Margaret's house was also proceeding slowly.

'How come I have to move the furniture?' said Susan. 'You said I could *be* in your movie.'

'Because *I'm* the director,' said Margaret. 'So I decide.'

'Margaret, you can be the monster in *my* film. No need for any make-up,' shouted Horrid Henry over the wall.

'Shut up, Henry,' said Margaret. 'Susan. Start walking down the path.'

'BOOOOOOOOOOOOO,' shouted Horrid Henry. 'BOOOOOOOOOOOOO.'

'Cut!' yelled Margaret. 'Quiet!' she screamed. 'I'm making a movie here.'

★

'Peter, hold the torch and shine the spotlight on me,' ordered Henry.

'Hold the torch?' said Peter.

'It's very important,' said Henry.

'Mum said you had to let me *be* in your movie,' said Peter. 'Or I'm telling on you.'

Horrid Henry glared at Perfect Peter.

Perfect Peter glared at Horrid Henry.

'Mum!' screamed Peter.

'Okay, you can be in the movie,' said Henry.

'Stop being horrid, Henry,' shouted Mum. 'Or you hand back that camera instantly.'

'I'm not being horrid; that's in the movie,' lied Henry.

Perfect Peter opened his mouth and then closed it.

'So what's my part?' said Peter.

★

Perfect Peter stood on the bench in the front garden.

'Now say your line, 'I am too horrible to live,' and jump off the bench into the crocodile-filled moat, where you are eaten alive and drown,' said Henry.

'I don't want to say that,' said Peter.

Horrid Henry lowered the camera. 'Do you want to be in the film or don't you?' he hissed.

'I am too horrible to live,' muttered Peter.

'Louder!' said Henry.

'I am too horrible to live,' said Peter, a fraction louder.

'And as you drown, scream out, "and I have smelly pants",' said Henry.

'*What?*' said Peter.

Tee hee, thought Horrid Henry.

'But how come you get to play all the other parts, *and* dance, *and* sing, and all I get to do is walk about going

wooooooo?' said Susan sourly in next
door's garden.

'Because it's *my* movie,' said Margaret.

'Keep it down, we're filming here,'
said Henry. 'Now Peter, you are walking
down the garden path out into the
street—'

'I thought I'd just drowned,' said Peter.

Henry rolled his eyes.

'No dummy, this is a horror film.
You *rose* from the dead, and now you're
walking down the path singing this song,
just before the hairy scary monster leaps
out of the bushes and rips you to shreds.

'Wibble bibble dribble pants
Bibble baby wibble pants
Wibble pants wibble pants
Dribble dribble dribble pants,'

sang Horrid Henry.

Perfect Peter hesitated. 'But Henry, why would my character sing that song?'

Henry glared at Peter.

'Because I'm the director and I say so,' said Henry.

Perfect Peter's lip trembled. He started walking.

'Wibble bibble dribble pants
Bibble baby wibble pants
Wibble pants wib—'

'I don't want to!' came a screech from next door's front garden.

'Susan, you *have* to be covered up in a sheet,' said Margaret.

'But no one will see my face and know it's me,' said Susan.

'Duh,' said Margaret. 'You're playing a ghost.'

Sour Susan flung off the sheet.

'Well I quit,' said Susan.

'You're fired!' shouted Margaret.

'I don't want to sing that dribble pants song,' said Peter.

'Then you're fired!' screamed Henry.

'No!' screamed Perfect Peter. 'I quit.' And he ran out of the front garden gate, shrieking and wailing.

Wow, thought Horrid Henry. He chased after Peter, filming.

'I've had it!' screamed Sour Susan. 'I don't want to be in your stupid film!'

She ran off down the road, shrieking and wailing.

Margaret chased after her, filming.

Cool, thought Horrid Henry, what a perfect end for his film, the puny wimp running off terrified—

BUMP!

Susan and Peter collided and sprawled flat on the pavement.

CRASH!

Henry and Margaret tripped over the screaming Peter and Susan.

SMASH!

Horrid Henry dropped his camcorder.

SMASH!

Moody Margaret dropped *her* camcorder.

OOPS.

Horrid Henry stared down at the twisted broken metal as his monster movie lay shattered on the concrete path.

WHOOPS.

Moody Margaret stared down at the cracked camcorder as her Hollywood horror film lay in pieces on the ground.

'Henry!' hissed Margaret.

'Margaret!' hissed Henry.

'This is all your fault!' they wailed.

Henry's Halloween Howlers

What was the name of the
little witch's brother?
He was cauld-Ron.

How many witches does it
take to change a lightbulb?
*Only one, but she changes
it into a toad.*

What do you do when fifty
zombies surround your house?
Hope it's Halloween.

RUDE RALPH: How do you
think they keep flies out
of the school canteen?
*HORRID HENRY: They
probably let them taste
the food!*

Henry's Halloween Howlers

What kind of jewellery
do witches wear?
Charm bracelets.

What do you call a
monster with a big hairy
nose, pointed yellow
teeth and red eyes?
Ugly.

What did one cool ghost
say to the other?
Get a life, dude.

Why didn't the
skeleton and the
monster fight?
*The skeleton didn't
have the guts.*

HORRID HENRY'S
FRIGHTENING
FUN

HALLOWEEN COUNTDOWN

Cross off the days on the calendar as you count down to the scariest, spookiest day of the year!

MONDAY	TUESDAY	WEDNESDAY	THURSDAY	FRIDAY	SATURDAY	SUNDAY
1	2	3	4	5	6	7
8	9	10	11	12	13	14
15	16	17	18	19	20	21
22	23	24	25	26	27	28
29	30	31				

OCTOBER

HORRID HENRY'S FAMILY'S AND FRIENDS' GREATEST FEARS

Peter
Leaving home without a hanky
Getting his clothes dirty
A day without homework
Being told off

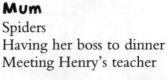

Mum
Spiders
Having her boss to dinner
Meeting Henry's teacher

Dad
Needles
Tomatoes
Meeting Henry's teacher

Stuck-Up Steve
Wearing second-hand clothes
Monsters under the bed

Rude Ralph
Meeting someone ruder than him

Moody Margaret
Being outwitted by Henry

Horrid Henry
Injections
Being outwitted by Margaret

Sour Susan
Margaret not being
her best friend anymore

GHOST SPOTTING

Here's a fun game for Halloween night.
Can you spot people dressed up in costumes
beginning with each of the letters below?

G_____

H_____

O_____

S_____

T_____

SWEET SEARCH

Now can you find people wearing costumes
beginning with every letter of one of
Horrid Henry's favourite sweets?

H_____

O_____

T_____

S_____

P_____

I_____

D_____

E_____

R_____

S_____

HOW SCARED ARE YOU?

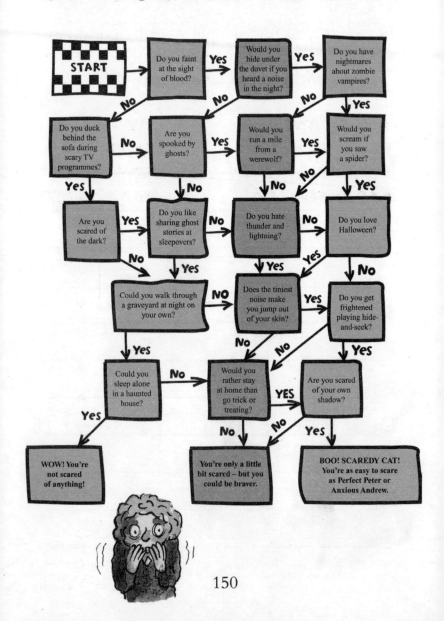

START

Do you faint at the sight of blood? — **Yes** → Would you hide under the duvet if you heard a noise in the night? — **Yes** → Do you have nightmares about zombie vampires?

No (from faint) ↓

No (from hide under duvet) ↓

No (from nightmares) → Do you have nightmares about zombie vampires? **Yes** ↓

Do you duck behind the sofa during scary TV programmes? ← **No** — Are you spooked by ghosts? — **Yes** → Would you run a mile from a werewolf? — **Yes** → Would you scream if you saw a spider?

Yes (duck behind sofa) ↓

No (spooked by ghosts) ↓

No (run a mile from werewolf) ↓

Yes (scream spider) ↓

Are you scared of the dark? — **Yes** → Do you like sharing ghost stories at sleepovers? — **No** → Do you hate thunder and lightning? — **No** → Do you love Halloween?

No (scared of dark) ↓

Yes (sharing ghost stories) ↓

Could you walk through a graveyard at night on your own? — **NO** → Does the tiniest noise make you jump out of your skin? — **Yes** → Do you get frightened playing hide-and-seek?

Yes (thunder and lightning) ↑

No (love Halloween) ↓

Yes (graveyard) ↓

No (tiniest noise) ↓

Yes (frightened hide-and-seek) ↓

Could you sleep alone in a haunted house? — **No** → Would you rather stay at home than go trick or treating? — **YES** → Are you scared of your own shadow?

No (tiniest noise) ↓

Yes (sleep alone) ↓

No (rather stay at home) ↓

No (scared of own shadow) ↓

Yes (scared of own shadow) ↓

WOW! You're not scared of anything!

You're only a little bit scared – but you could be braver.

BOO! SCAREDY CAT! You're as easy to scare as Perfect Peter or Anxious Andrew.

TERRIBLE TEENS

Find the names of some terrible teens in the wordsearch puzzle below, including Horrid Henry's beastly babysitters!

ANGRY ANNA

CRABBY CHRIS

MELLOW MARTIN

RABID REBECCA

TETCHY TESS

FILTHY PHIL

MOULDY MYRA

TORNADO TARIQ

CLUE:
All the words are hidden separately, like ANGRY and ANNA.

151

TRICK OR TREAT!

Halloween is the perfect time for playing
tricky tricks on your enemies. Try some
of Henry's favourite tricks below.

1. Leave a telephone message for your
parents, saying: 'Call Mr Lyon about
an urgent matter.' Leave the telephone
number for them to ring your nearest zoo.

2. Put salt in your hair, and tell your
mum you've got dandruff.

3. Make some silly stickers, saying things like 'I'm a Worm!' or 'I love Miss Battle-Axe' and stick them on people's backs.

4. At breakfast time, when no one is looking, swap your annoying brother's or sister's hard-boiled egg for a raw one.

5. Turn the clocks backwards or forwards so that everybody gets up far too early or far too late.

HORRID HENRY GHOSTS AND GHOULS

SPOOKY SLEEPOVER MAZE

Henry has lost the rest of his class during
a sleepover in the Old Town Museum.
Can you help him find them?

START

154

MONSTROUS MENUS

Can you work out which of the tasty
treats in the list below belongs
to which menu?

~~Snooty Snails~~
~~Spooky Spookhetti~~

~~Snobby Salmon~~
~~Phantom Fries~~

Ghostly Gobble and Go
1. Banshee Burgers
2. Ice Screaming
3. Phantom Fries
4. spooky spookhetti

CLUE:
Look for a tasty treat
to eat with burgers,
and a scary
pasta dish.

Restaurant Le Posh
1. Best Beetroot Mousse
2. Luxury Lemon Sorbet
3. Snobby salmon
4. snooty snails

CLUE:
Both of these posh
treats are a bit fishy!

155

SPOOKY JOKES CRISS-CROSS

Match the words below to these well-known spooky jokes, then fit them into the criss-cross puzzle! One word has already been filled in.

~~GUTS~~   ~~BODY~~   ~~NECK~~

~~MOUSE~~   ~~BLOOD~~   ~~COFFIN~~

~~SCREAM~~   ~~CACKLE~~   ~~TICKLERS~~

Why didn't the skeleton cross the road?
He had no G U T S .

Why didn't the skeleton go to the party?
He had no B O D Y *to go with.*

Which jokes do skeletons like?
Rib T I C K L E R S .

What's it like to be kissed by a vampire?
It's a pain in the N E C K .

When is it unlucky to see a black cat?
When you're a M O U S E .

Why are graveyards so noisy?
Because of all the **C O F F I N** .

What noise does witches' cereal make?
Snap, C A C K L E *and pop.*

What's Dracula's favourite soup?
S C R E A M *of tomato.*

Where do vampires keep their money?
In B L O O D *banks.*

CLUE:
Fill in the longest
word first!

SCARY MOVIE MONSTER PARTY

Check out Henry's top three
ingredients for the best scary movie
birthday party ever . . .

1. INVITATIONS

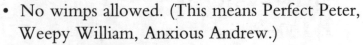

- Invite all the best people.
- Send to Rude Ralph,
  Tough Toby and Beefy Bert.
- No wimps allowed. (This means Perfect Peter,
  Weepy William, Anxious Andrew.)
- Definitely NO girls.

2. MONSTROUS MUNCHIES

- Make sure we have the best snacks ever!

3. SCARY MONSTER GAMES

- Play some wicked games — and make sure you win!

EYEBALL SPOON RACE

You will need:

A spoon for every player
A ping-pong ball for
every player
Permanent marker pens
of any colour

Instructions:

1. Tell everyone to draw a dot on their ping-pong ball to turn it into a scary monster eyeball.

2. Mark out the start and finish lines for your race.

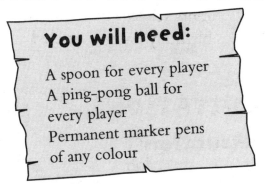

3. Stand on the start line, balancing your monster eyeball on your spoon — along with the other players.

4. The first person to reach the finish line without dropping their monster eyeball . . . is the WINNER!

MONSTER PASS THE PARCEL

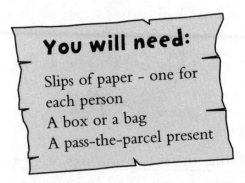

You will need:

Slips of paper - one for each person
A box or a bag
A pass-the-parcel present

Instructions:

1. Put an 'M' for Monster on one of the slips of paper. Leave the other slips blank, then fold them all up and put them in your box or bag.

2. Turn on some spooky music and gather everyone in a circle.

3. Each player picks out a slip of paper without showing it to anyone else. The one who get the 'M' is the Monster.

4. Start playing Pass the Parcel.

5. While the game is going on the person who is the Monster must try to kill as many people as possible without being caught. (To kill someone, the Monster has to stick their tongue out at them, without being spotted by the others.)

6. If you are killed, you have to lie down on the floor. But if anyone works out who the Monster is, the game is over, and that person wins the Pass the Parcel prize.

7. If the Monster kills everyone before the Parcel is opened, the Monster gets the prize.

HORRID HENRY'S SPECIAL EFFECTS TRICK

Horrid Henry has a favourite special effect he uses to trick his family and friends during Halloween.

It makes it look as though a monster is spitting out deadly venom into its victim's eye. This is brilliant for scaring parents.

VICIOUS VENOM

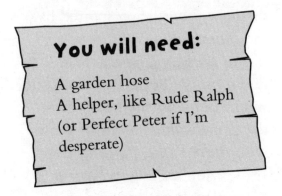

You will need:

A garden hose
A helper, like Rude Ralph
(or Perfect Peter if I'm
desperate)

What I do:

1. Ralph hides in the garden with the garden hose.

2. I turn the water on so it sprays out of the hose, then start shouting 'HELP! THERE'S A MONSTER IN THE GARDEN!' so my parents come rushing out of the house.

3. From his hiding place, Ralph sprays the water at my face so that it looks as if the monster is squirting venom into my eyes.

4. I scream more loudly, 'DEADLY VENOM! OUCH!' and roll around on the ground in pain, rubbing my eyes.

MONSTROUS MAKEOVERS

Check out some of Henry's easiest scary
costumes for Halloween – or any time!

GHOST

1. Take an old white sheet and cut a
    hole in the middle to put your head
    through.
2. Paint your face with white paint,
    with black around your eyes.
3. Put white talcum powder in your
    hair to give a ghostly effect.

166

MUMMY

1. Use bandages or an old white sheet cut up into long strips. If you're really stuck, you can use toilet roll.

2. Put on plain white clothes, like a T-shirt and trousers.

3. Wrap the bandages, sheet strips or toilet roll around you. Pin carefully to your clothes with safety pins when you need to start a new piece.

4. Paint your face with white face paint, and just wrap a few bandages around your head, so you can see where you're going.

HOW TO MAKE A HORRID HANGER

Henry puts a horrible hanger on his bedroom door to scare Perfect Peter away. Follow the instructions and see if you can make your door hanger as scary as Horrid Henry's.

You will need:

Cardboard or paper
Glue (if you are using paper)
Scissors
Pencils, pens or paints

Instructions:

1. Copy the door hanger shape onto your cardboard or paper and cut it out. If you're using paper, cut out two copies of the template and glue them together. This will make your door hanger stronger. But don't do any writing or decoration until the glue is dry.

2. Write a message on your door hanger. You can put a different message on each side, for example:

> Side 1: ENTER AT YOUR PERIL! or PRIVATE! KEEP OUT!
> Side 2: WELCOME! or PLEASE COME IN!

3. Remember to turn your door hanger to the correct side or you might frighten away your friends.

4. If you like, you can decorate your door hanger with pictures or patterns.

COULD *YOU* TURN INTO A TEACHER?

There aren't many things Horrid Henry
thinks are scariest than having Moody
Margaret to stay, except for getting a
horrible disease that turns you
into a TEACHER.

Are YOU in danger of catching
a deadly case of Teacher–itis?

1. Are you wearing any of the following?

a) A saggy, baggy old cardigan
b) Sensible, brown, lace-up shoes
c) Neither of the above

2. If your friends are making lots of noise, what do you do?

a) Shout 'Shut up! I can't hear myself
think,' at them
b) Try to think of a game that isn't so noisy
c) Join in and make even more noise than them

3. How do you treat your little brothers and sisters?

a) Tell them very firmly that, 'small children should be seen and not heard'

b) Encourage them with kind words, like 'Well done' and 'Aren't you clever?'

c) Call them 'worms' and ban them from joining any games

4. The house is a mess, but your parents are just watching TV. What do you do?

a) Tell them that they're lazy, and the house is a disgrace

b) Suggest that they finish all the housework first, and that their reward will be an hour of TV

c) Sneak off when they're not looking, and make even more mess

How to score:

For every (a) score 3 points; for every (b) score 2 points; for every (c) score 0 points. Look at the back of the book for what your score means.

TERRIFYING 'T' WORDS

How many words can you think of that start
with the letter T? Bonus points for words
that describe something scary!

1 _Torcher_   6 _____

2 _Toren gost_ 7 _____

3 _____   8 _____

4 _____   9 _____

5 _____   10 _____

GROSS FOOD WORD MUDDLE

How many words can you make using only the letters from one of Horrid Henry's most disgusting foods?

CAULIFLOWER CHEESE

1 _____

2 _____

3 _____

4 _____

5 _____

6 _____

7 _____

8 _____

9 _____

10 _____

CRISS–CROSS CONQUEROR

When Horrid Henry attacks Moody Margaret or Perfect Peter, he's not a boy any more, he's a dragon or a shark or an alien. Find some of his wildest daydreams below.

4 letters
~~CRAB~~
~~BULL~~

5 letters
~~SHARK~~
~~ALIEN~~

6 letters
~~PIRATE~~
~~DRAGON~~

7 letters
~~WARRIOR~~
~~MONSTER~~
~~OCTOPUS~~
~~VAMPIRE~~

8 letters
~~ELEPHANT~~

9 letters
~~CROCODILE~~

CLUE:
Fill in the longest
word first!

175

CODE CRACKING

When Greasy Greta, the demon dinner
lady, starts pinching all the tasty treats from
Horrid Henry's lunch, it's time for revenge.

Crack the code and discover his plan.

HE MAKES YET
G D   L Z J D R   G N S

CHILLI
B G H K K H

BISCUITS
A H R B T H S R

CLUE:
Replace every letter
here with the next
letter from the
alphabet.

GETTING FROM A-Z

Can you change the first word to the last
word by only changing one letter at a time?
Each word in the middle has to be
a real word!

DARK

BARK

_____

_____

RATS

ROTS

BEAT THE BOGEY BABYSITTER

Horrid Henry hates babysitters – especially Rabid Rebecca, the toughest teen in town. He just wants to be left alone to watch TV and eat crisps all night. Could you beat the bogey babysitter or would you be sent to bed early? Take the quiz and then check your answers at the back of the book to find out.

1. Do you like having a babysitter?
   a) Yes, as long as it's somebody nice
   b) It's okay, but I miss Mum and Dad when they go out
   c) No! I'm not a baby and I don't need to be sat on by a bossy teenager

2. What would your ideal babysitter be like?

   a) She'd play games with me and read me stories
   b) She'd help me if I asked her
   c) She'd let me stay up all night and eat sweets until I was sick

3. When Rabid Rebecca first arrives, how would you show her who's boss?

a) I wouldn't, because she'd be in charge

b) I'd sneak the biscuit tin up to my bedroom

c) I'd hide her homework and 'accidentally' pour orange juice down the front of her new jeans

4. How would you annoy Rabid Rebecca when she's watching TV?

a) Ask her politely if she'd mind changing channels

b) Munch crisps very loudly in her ear

c) Dance in front of the TV, blocking her view and singing as loudly as you can

5. What would you do if you didn't want Rabid Rebecca to babysit again?

a) I'd stick my tongue out at her when she wasn't looking

b) I'd play loud music in my bedroom

c) I'd flood the bathroom

FIND THE HALLOWEEN PAIRS

Horrid Henry sets out to scare
on Halloween night!
Can you find the four matching pairs?

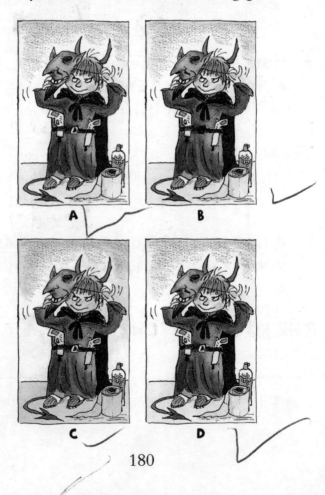

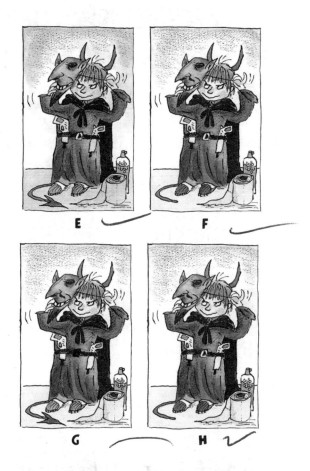

THE FOUR MATCHING PAIRS ARE:

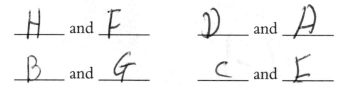

H and F   D and A

B and G   C and E

181

MAKE A WICKED WATERBOMB

This waterbomb is fantastic for attacking a rival. It's quite tricky to make at first, but it's easy once you know how.

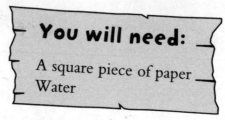

You will need:

A square piece of paper
Water

Instructions:

1. Fold your square from corner to corner, to crease, as shown in the diagram

2. Push in the sides to create a triangle

3. Fold up the corners to the point at the top. Turn over and repeat on the other side

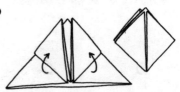

4. Fold in the sides.
Turn over and
repeat on the
other side.

5. From the top, fold
each of the flaps down
and tuck into the sides,
as shown. Turn over
and repeat on the other
side. Don't worry if
they don't fit very neatly.

6. Gently pull your
waterbomb into shape,
then blow hard into the
hole at the top.

BLOW
INTO
HOLE

7. Fill with water – and
throw very quickly!

FILL
WITH
WATER

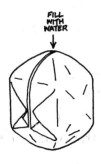

ZOMBIES!
VAMPIRES! GHOSTS!

Halloween is packed with creepy creatures.
What five monsters would you *not* want
to meet on a dark, dark night?

1 Zombies

2 Vampires

3 Ghosts

4 The dark creep

5 witch

184

SCARY COSTUMES

Sometimes monsters can be fun –
if you're the one who is doing the
scaring! What five monsters would
you most like to dress up as for
Halloween?

1 _____

2 _____

3 _____

4 _____

5 _____

WHICH HALLOWEEN HORROR ARE YOU?

1. What kind of clothes would you wear on Halloween?

a) Anything torn and dirty
b) A white sheet
c) A long black velvet coat
d) A long black dress and a tall black hat
e) Something pink and fluffy

2. What's your favourite treat?

a) Chocolate fingers
b) Marshmallows
c) Neck-tarines
d) Sand-witches
e) Tangerines

3. What's your best trick?

a) Stuffing a glove with cotton wool, shaking hands with your victim and leaving your hand behind

b) Tapping on the window and shouting 'whoooooo'

c) Dripping fake blood from your mouth

d) Waving your wand and turning your friend into a frog

e) Saying 'boo!' quietly, and running away

4. What do you like best about Halloween?

a) Scaring people in the streets

b) Haunting your friends and family

c) Escaping from your coffin for the night

d) Flying around on your broomstick

e) Having fun with friends

How to score:

Count up how many (a)'s, (b)'s, (c)'s, (d)'s and (e)'s you got, then check the answer guide at the back.

CREEPY CRAZY CREATURES

Horrid Henry often imagines he's a fire-breathing dragon burning his prey to a crisp or a coiling cobra about to strike.

If he could cast spells, he'd turn that goody-goody Peter into a beetle or a toad.

Why not turn yourself or someone you know into a crazy creature? You could copy one of the pictures on this page or draw a completely new creature.

FOUL FOODS

Yeuch! Can you find the foul foods
in the criss-cross puzzle?

5 letters
~~LIVER~~
~~SQUID~~

6 letters
~~SNAILS~~

11 letters
~~CAULIFLOWER~~

7 letters
~~SPINACH~~
~~OYSTERS~~
~~MUSSELS~~

8 letters
~~BEETROOT~~

CLUE:
Fill in the longest
word first!

AUTUMN CROSSWORD

Perfect Peter enjoys long nature walks to look at the different coloured leaves in autumn. Henry prefers Halloween, bonfire night and throwing lots of leaves at Peter! Test your knowledge of Autumn with this quick crossword.

4→BrOWN

(handwritten crossword answers)

1 ACORN
2 CONKEr
3 CANDLE
5 SPArKLEr
6 rE
7 WHEEL

192

ACROSS

1. The fruit of an oak tree.—
5. A firework you can hold in your—
   hand
6. The colour of hawthorn berries —→
7. A firework that spins round is called a
   Catherine _ _ _ _ _.

DOWN

2. The fruit of a chestnut tree. ⌣
3. Another sort of firework is a Roman ↶
   ~~orange~~
4. Leaves can turn this colour in the—
   Autumn.

HORRID HENRY'S ZOMBIE VAMPIRE RESOLUTIONS

1. Expose Miss Battle-Axe for the zombie vampire she is

2. Tell Peter there's a monster in his wardrobe and a zombie under his bed

3. Make the scariest horror movie ever, called 'The Undead Demon Monster Who Would Not Die'

4. Turn Margaret into a zombie . . . wait, she already is one – tee hee!

5. Round up all the zombie vampires in the neighbourhood and herd them towards the school. Ha! That should give me a few extra days holiday . . .

CREEPY-CRAWLY PIZZA

Horrid Henry loves pizza and hates having to share it with Perfect Peter. So Henry makes sure that Peter won't want even a bite – by creating his own terrible topping. Here's how.

You will need:

A pizza base
Chopped tomatoes
Black olives
Red and yellow peppers
Cheese
Anchovies (if you like them)

Instructions:

1. Spread the pizza base with the tomatoes.
2. Sprinkle with grated cheese or lay on slices of mozzarella cheese.
3. Put black olives on top.
4. Cut the red and yellow pepper into thin slices and arrange them around the black olives so that they look like legs.
5. If you are using anchovies too, place them on the pizza, in squiggly shapes to look like creepy-crawlies.
6. Ask a grown-up to cook the pizza for you.
7. When the pizza is placed on the table, shout:

Yuck! It's covered in blood!

Gross-Out! Wiggly Worms!

Ugh! Creepy-Crawlies!

Goodbye, Gruesome gang!

ANSWERS

p151

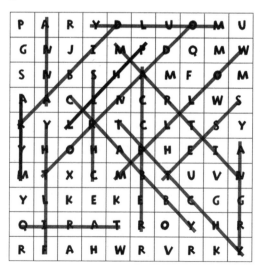

p154

START

p155

Ghostly Gobble and Go:
Phantom Fries
Spooky Spookhetti

Restaurant Le Posh:
Snooty Snails
Snobby Salmon

p156–157

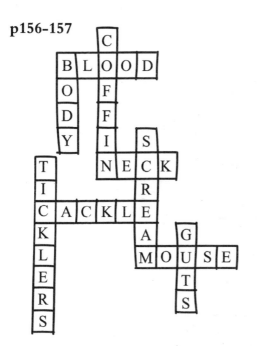

p158–159

Can you find Horrid Henry hiding at the Haunted House?

p170–171

8 – 12

Uh-oh! You've caught the deadly disease and there's no cure. You're going to turn into a teacher – as grumpy and grouchy as Miss Battle-Axe.

5 – 8

Watch out! You're in the danger zone. Get help now – before it's too late.

1 – 4

Phew! You're safe from this horrible disease. There's no chance of your getting Teacher-itis!

p174–175

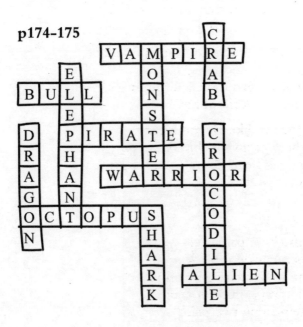

p176

He makes hot chilli biscuits

p177

DARK – BARK – BARS – BATS – RATS – ROTS

p178–179

Mostly (a)'s: You're a babysitter's dream – well-behaved and polite, just like Perfect Peter. Someone as mean and moody as Rabid Rebecca would have you tucked up in bed without any supper, way before bedtime.

Mostly (b)'s: You might scare off a timid teenager, but not the snarling Rabid Rebecca. You'll need to be a lot noisier and naughtier to get rid of her.

Mostly (c)'s: Just like Horrid Henry, you know how to give Rabid Rebecca an evening she'll never forget – and she'll certainly never be back.

p180–181

The four matching pairs are:
B and G (belt buckle is black)
C and E (no moustache on mask)
F and H (no point on devil's tail)
A and D (remaining two pairs!)

p186–187

p188–189

Mostly (a)'s: You're a brilliant brain-munching zombie!

Mostly (b)'s: You're a spooky spine-tingling ghost – whooooo-ooooooooo!

Mostly (c)'s: You're a fangtastically vicious vampire.

Mostly (d)'s: You're a spellbinding wicked witch.

Mostly (e)'s: You're a perfectly pink fluffy bunny!

p191

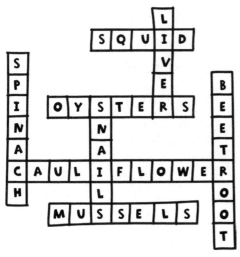

p192-193

Storybooks

Early Readers

Don't be Horrid Henry
Horrid Henry's Birthday Party
Horrid Henry's Holiday
Horrid Henry's Underpants
Horrid Henry Gets Rich Quick
Horrid Henry and the Football Fiend
Horrid Henry's Nits
Horrid Henry and Moody Margaret
Horrid Henry's Thank You Letter
Horrid Henry Car Journey
Moody Margaret's School
Horrid Henry's Tricks and Treats
Horrid Henry's Rainy Day
Horrid Henry's Author Visit
Horrid Henry Meets the Queen
Horrid Henry's Sports Day
Moody Margaret Casts a Spell

Colour Books

Horrid Henry's Big Bad Book
Horrid Henry's Wicked Ways
Horrid Henry's Evil Enemies
Horrid Henry Rules the World
Horrid Henry's House of Horrors
Horrid Henry's Dreadful Deeds
Horrid Henry Shows Who's Boss
Horrid Henry's A-Z of Everything Horrid
Horrid Henry's Fearsome Four
Horrid Henry's Royal Riot
Horrid Henry's Tricky Tricks
Horrid Henry's Lucky Dip

Joke Books

Horrid Henry's Joke Book
Horrid Henry's Jolly Joke Book
Horrid Henry's Mighty Joke Book
Horrid Henry versus Moody Margaret
Horrid Henry's Hilariously Horrid Joke Book
Horrid Henry's Purple Hand Gang Joke Book
Horrid Henry's All Time Favourite Joke Book
Horrid Henry's Jumbo Joke Book

Activity Books

Horrid Henry's Brainbusters
Horrid Henry's Headscratchers
Horrid Henry's Mindbenders
Horrid Henry's Colouring Book
Horrid Henry's Puzzle Book
Horrid Henry's Sticker Book
Horrid Henry Runs Riot
Horrid Henry's Classroom Chaos
Horrid Henry's Holiday Havoc
Horrid Henry's Wicked Wordsearches
Horrid Henry's Mad Mazes
Horrid Henry's Crazy Crosswords
Horrid Henry's Big Bad Puzzle Book
Horrid Henry's Gold Medal Games
Where's Horrid Henry?
Horrid Henry's Crafty Christmas
Where's Horrid Henry Colouring Book

Fact Books

Horrid Henry's Ghosts
Horrid Henry's Dinosaurs
Horrid Henry's Sports
Horrid Henry's Food
Horrid Henry's King and Queens
Horrid Henry's Bugs
Horrid Henry's Animals
Horrid Henry's Ghosts
Horrid Henry's Crazy Creatures

**Visit Horrid Henry's website at
www.horridhenry.co.uk for competitions,
games, downloads and a monthly newsletter**

HORRID HENRY

The first book about the adventures
of Horrid Henry, in which Henry tries
(unbelievably) to be good, goes to dance
classes, makes 'Glop' with Moody
Margaret and goes on holiday.

'Henry is a truly
great character'
Sunday Times

WHERE'S HORRID HENRY?

Featuring 32 pages of things to spot, join
Henry and his friends (and evilest enemies!)
on their awesome adventures – from
birthday parties and camping trips
to hiding out at a spooky haunted house.
With a challenging checklist of things to
find, this is Henry's most horrid
challenge yet!

The question is, where's Horrid Henry?

HORRID HENRY'S CANNIBAL CURSE

The final collection of four brand new utterly horrid stories in which Horrid Henry triumphantly reveals his guide to perfect parents, reads an interesting book about a really naughty girl, and conjures up the cannibal's curse to deal with his enemies and small, annoying brother.